W9-AIP-934

Jack Quack

by Lucy Nolan

illustrated by Andrea Wesson

Marshall Cavendish • New York

Text copyright © 2001 by Lucy Nolan
Illustrations copyright © 2001 by Andrea Wesson
All rights reserved
Marshall Cavendish, 99 White Plains Road,
Tarrytown, NY 10591

Library of Congress Cataloging-in-Publication Data
Nolan, Lucy A.
Jack Quack / Lucy Nolan.
    p.   cm.
Summary: When an awkward duckling named Otis
assumes a new identity as Jack Quack, Renegade
Drake, he wins new respect from his family and friends.
ISBN0-76145153-6
[1. Ducks—Fiction. 2. Self-esteem—Fiction. 3. Ani-
mals—Infancy—Fiction.] I. Title.
PZ7.N688 Jac 2001
[E]—dc21   00-064515

The text of this book is set in 16 point Veljovic Book.
The illustrations are rendered in pen and ink and
watercolor.
Printed in Hong Kong

First Marshall Cavendish paperback edition 2003

6 5 4 3 2 1

www.marshallcavendish.com

*To Dylan, Carson,
Benjamin, Daniel,
Luke, Cameron,
and Connor*
—L. N.

To Herman
—A. W.

eep in the Silverthorn Forest, on the shores of a cool green lake, lived a family of mallards with seven fine sons. There were Reed, Willow, Forrest, Juniper, Hawthorne, and Woodruff.

And then there was Otis.

Every morning the young drakes lined up for their lessons. But Otis found life too interesting to pay attention for very long.

"Paddle your feet," their mother said.

Reed and Willow paddled hard and became strong swimmers.

But Otis always got distracted by the tadpoles and missed the end of the lesson.

"*Above* the water, Otis!" his mother said. "Swim *above* the water."

During flying lessons, Forrest and Juniper learned to rise gracefully into the air. But before Otis got very far, he always noticed the hummingbirds.

"Pay attention, Otis!" his mother scolded. "Foxes love ducklings who don't pay attention."

For a moment, the thought of sharp teeth and beady eyes made Otis fly higher. But before long, he was trying to hover among the flowers again.

On this very same lake lived a pretty young duck named Violet.

Hawthorne and Woodruff strutted along the shore to show just how handsome they had become. Reed and Willow swam lazy circles, while Forrest and Juniper soared above. Even shy Otis was smitten by the lovely Violet.

But Violet drifted alone among the lilies, dreaming of the daring duck who would take her to live in the moat of a castle.

As the summer went by, all of the young drakes lost interest in Violet. All but Otis, that is.

Otis adored Violet, but he was much too bashful to speak to her. Instead, he spent his days suffering in silence. Well, except for the time he tried to peck their names into a tree. That made quite a racket and gave him an awful headache as well.

One fall day, Otis began to feel a little brave and picked a pretty bouquet.

Otis had paid attention during flying lessons, but he had never listened during *landing* lessons. He toppled into the mud and slid all the way to Violet's feet.

Violet giggled. Then she laughed until she fell into the clover.

Otis was so embarrassed that he turned and ran. Deeper and deeper into the forest he went, until the sound of Violet's laughter faded away.

As the days went by, the breeze turned chilly and the leaves swirled down. Only when the snow came did Otis swallow his pride and go home.

But by then, the ducks
had flown south, and the
wind howled across
the frozen lake.

Otis spent a long
miserable winter alone,
deep in the Silverthorn
Forest.

When the wind began to lose its bite, Otis knew he could soon return to the lake. But this time, nobody would dare to laugh at him. For during the long lonely nights, Otis had devised a clever plan.

He gathered leaves to make a mask, and wove a cap of reeds. And for a dashing touch, he plucked a tailfeather from his rump, which left him feeling rather cross.

One morning, Otis awoke to the feel of the warm spring sun, and his heart leapt. It was time to go home.

Otis watched as the ducks settled in. Most of the ducklings from the year before now had ducklings of their own. Only Violet remained alone.

All the ducks were on the shore, quacking, when Otis made his grand entrance. As he wobbled and skidded to shore, the ducks cried, "You saved our ducklings!"

"I did?" Otis asked, and turned to see three dizzy bullfrogs. "Well, of course I did! I'm Jack Quack, Renegade Drake. Prince of the Forest, King of the Lake."

And with that, he flew away, leaving the ducks to stare in wonder.

The next day, the ducks were fussing again, so Otis hopped on a log for a better look. The log began to roll, and Otis flapped his feet faster and faster, trying not to fall. The ducks scattered, leaving two snapping turtles in his path.

As the turtles went tumbling, Otis dusted himself off and said, "I *meant* to do that. Because I'm Jack Quack, Renegade Drake. Prince of the Forest, King of the Lake."

As tales of his derring-do spread, Jack Quack became the most popular duck on the lake. For several days, he enjoyed the glory.

After awhile, though, Otis longed to tell his brothers who he really was. But if he did that, surely nobody would pay attention to him any more.

One afternoon, when Otis was telling of the great dangers he had faced, the ducks began to squawk frantically.

Across the lake, Otis saw Violet gazing at her reflection. And behind her, a fox crept slowly along the dock.

"Save her!" the ducks begged Otis.

Otis didn't know what to do. Oh, how Otis wished he had the speed of Juniper, or the courage of Hawthorne or Woodruff.

But Otis couldn't let anything happen to his lovely Violet! He flew across the lake and landed on the dock with a thud. To his surprise, the fox rocketed overhead.

Otis suddenly found himself staring into Violet's eyes. "I—I'm Jack Quack," he stuttered, "Renegade Drake—"

"No, you're not," Violet said with a giggle. "You're Otis."

Otis's feathers drooped. "I guess I'm nothing but a silly duck, after all," he said.

"That's what I like about you!" Violet cried. "You make me laugh! And, Otis," she added, fluttering her eyelashes, "you're my hero."

Otis and Violet fell in love and went to live on a millpond that they thought was a moat. Violet had the life that she dreamed of, for exciting things always happened around Otis.

After all, he was Jack Quack, Renegade Drake. Prince of the Forest, King of the Lake.